JOIN THE FUN
IN CABIN SIX . . .

KATIE is the perfect team player. She loves competitive games, planned activities, and coming up with her own great ideas.

MEGAN would rather lose herself in fantasyland than get into organized fun.

SARAH would be much happier if she could spend her time reading instead of exerting herself.

ERIN is much more interested in boys, clothes, and makeup than in playing kids' games at camp.

TRINA hates conflicts ~~~~ ust wants everyone to b~~~~

AND THEY ARE! ~~~~ differences, the Cabi~~~~ having the time of their lives a~~~~ SUNNYSIDE!

Look for More Fun and Games with
CAMP SUNNYSIDE FRIENDS
by Marilyn Kaye
from Avon Books

And Don't Miss
My Camp Memory Book
*the delightful souvenir album for
recording camp memories and planning activities*

Coming Soon

(#14) Megan's Ghost

MARILYN KAYE is the author of many popular books for young readers, including the "Out of This World" series and the "Sisters" books. She is an associate professor at St. John's University and lives in Brooklyn, New York.

Camp Sunnyside is the camp Marilyn Kaye wishes that she had gone to every summer when she was a kid.

CAMP SUNNYSIDE FRIENDS #13

Big Sister Blues

Marilyn Kaye

AN AVON  CAMELOT BOOK

CAMP SUNNYSIDE FRIENDS #13: BIG SISTER BLUES is an original publication of Avon Books. This work has never before appeared in book form.

AVON BOOKS
A division of
The Hearst Corporation
1350 Avenue of the Americas
New York, New York 10019

Copyright © 1991 by Marilyn Kaye
Published by arrangement with the author
Library of Congress Catalog Card Number: 91-91789
ISBN: 0-380-76551-9
RL: 5.2

First Avon Camelot Printing: August 1991

CAMELOT TRADEMARK REG. U.S. PAT. OFF. AND IN OTHER COUNTRIES, MARCA REGISTRADA, HECHO EN U.S.A.

Printed in the U.S.A.

OPM 10 9 8 7 6 5 4 3 2 1

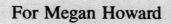

For Megan Howard

Chapter 1

Sarah Fine let out a heavy sigh and put her head down on her pillow. It had been raining for almost two days straight, and there was no sign that it would be stopping anytime soon. And, as if the rainstorm outside wasn't depressing enough, Sarah was trying to write a letter, and she was experiencing a first-class case of writer's block, which for her was pretty unusual. The only thing she loved more than writing was reading.

Megan Lindsay peeked up at the bunk above her. "What's wrong?" she asked. Sarah figured her sigh must have been much louder than she had intended to jolt Megan out of one of her daydreams. That was the first thing she'd said in about half an hour.

Sarah lifted her head. "I've been trying to

1

write this letter to my dad and my sister, Alison, and I just don't think it's very interesting."

"Why are you so worried about a letter to your family?" Erin Chapman asked, taking a break to let the first coat of polish on her toenails dry. She was sitting on her bed with a cotton ball stuck between each toe. "I never write mine."

"But your's are traveling all over in Europe. You wouldn't know where to send a letter to them," Sarah said. "Besides, they usually just send you postcards. Alison and Dad always write me great letters. I can't wait to get them." By then, Erin had stopped listening and was back to painting her toenails.

"Why don't you tell us what you've got so far and we'll help you," Trina Sandberg suggested. She and Katie Dillon were playing Monopoly, and Trina had just placed a hotel on Boardwalk.

Sarah sat up and dangled her legs off her bunk. "Well, first I told Alison how sorry I am that she lost her job at the community center." She looked at her friends. "She was going to use the money she earned to buy a

2

computer for college, but at the last minute the center decided they could afford to use only volunteers," Sarah explained.

"That's awful," Trina said. "What's she going to do now?"

"I don't know. Alison says most places have already finished hiring students for the summer." Sarah felt bad for her older sister. She knew how important getting that computer was to her.

"I bet Alison's found a job by the time she gets your letter," Megan told Sarah in a cheery voice.

"Maybe," Sarah said.

Katie threw the dice across the Monopoly board. "Did you tell her we beat Eagle in ultimate Frisbee last week?" she asked.

Sarah nodded. "Yeah, she was really excited to hear how it turned out since the Sunnyside girls *always* creamed the Eagle boys when she was here." Sarah didn't like to participate in athletic competitions, but she was always an enthusiastic fan of the Sunnyside girls' teams.

"Then I told her about the going-away party everyone's having for Deedee," Sarah said. "And how I'll be sorry when she's not around

anymore, but I won't be sorry about ..."
Sarah cued her friends.

"No more archery!" the girls shouted. Ever since Ms. Winkle had announced that Deedee, the archery counselor, would be leaving the camp, Sarah had talked nonstop about how happy she'd be when they didn't have to take archery anymore.

Katie handed her remaining Monopoly money over to Trina and said, "Darn! We're even now—two games to two games." She turned to Sarah and Megan while Trina began putting the game away. "I don't see why Deedee has to leave just because her parents decided to move," Katie said. Sarah couldn't tell if she was angry about losing or about Deedee's leaving.

"Deedee says they bought a big farm, and they need her help," Trina explained.

"I wonder who Ms. Winkle will get to replace her," Megan said. "I hope whoever it is knows tennis. My game could use a lot of help." Megan was the best tennis player at Sunnyside, but she was always trying to improve so that she could beat her friend Stewart from Camp Eagle.

"I think it would be neat to have something

4

a little different—like gymnastics," Trina suggested.

Sarah looked down at her stocky body and tried to imagine herself doing backbends, somersaults, and handsprings. "That would be different all right—so different I don't think my body would ever forgive me. What about something less stressful—like creative writing?" she said.

"Creative writing?" Erin made a face. "What could be more stressful than that? With all the chlorine in the pool and the sweating we have to do, what this camp needs is someone to teach skin and hair care and beauty techniques." She looked around at the others. "I know several girls at Sunnyside who would certainly benefit from a few lessons."

Of course, Sarah knew Erin was referring to the cabin six girls. She'd always been more concerned with her appearance than her cabin mates. She spent most of her free time putting on makeup, brushing her hair, or trying on new outfits.

"I know," Katie said. "Everybody, write down your ideas for the suggestion box." The suggestion box was located outside the dining hall, and the cabin six girls had used it more than once to try to get a few items removed from the Camp Sunnyside menu. "Maybe if Ms. Winkle hasn't already selected someone to replace Deedee, she'll keep our recommendations in mind when she does."

Erin waved her right hand in the air. "Count me out," she said. "My second coat isn't dry yet."

The others ignored Erin. They were used to her not wanting to do the same things they did. "Don't you think Ms. Winkle's already picked someone?" Trina asked. "The party's tonight, and Deedee's catching the earliest bus out of here tomorrow morning."

"You know Ms. Winkle. If she'd picked someone, we'd have heard about it," Katie said. "She lives for those kinds of announcements."

"Katie's right," Megan agreed. "It couldn't hurt to make a few suggestions."

"Well, it could hurt me," Sarah said. "For my sake, please just don't put down anything like football or wrestling."

"Aren't you going to help us?" Trina asked.

"No, you guys better do it without me," Sarah said. "I don't think Ms. Winkle's going to go for anything like American literature or poetry writing."

As the other girls pulled out scraps of paper and scribbled their ideas down, Sarah folded her letter, put it in an envelope, and sealed the flap. After all, a short letter was better than no letter at all. And there'd probably be more to report in the next week's letter anyway.

Sarah pulled her novel *Through the Crystal Mirror* from under her pillow, opened it up to the marked page, and rolled over on her stomach once again. She was at the part in the book where the heroine, Linda Stanfield, had an argument with her twin sister. As Linda sat in her room plotting revenge, a gust of wind blew through the bedroom window, and carried Linda into a magical world through the mirror. Within seconds, Sarah was out of cabin six and traveling through the book's pages with Linda.

That night, the cabin six girls were in charge of decorating the dining hall for Deedee's going-away party. Trina had thought of an "Old MacDonald" theme, so they'd bought craft supplies when they'd gone to Pine Ridge earlier in the week. Donna, the arts and crafts counselor, had every camper make papier mâché farm animals during class. Bent pink pipe cleaners became curly pig tails and cotton balls covered the sheep's body.

"These are great," Megan said as she pulled the animals out of bags.

"Yeah. Everyone really went all out for Deedee," Sarah said. "This is going to be the best Sunnyside party yet."

"Someone help me with these streamers," Katie said. "Did anyone remember to bring tape?"

Trina reached into a paper bag. "Here it is," she said triumphantly. "I'll get a chair and help you hang them."

Sarah and Megan blew up the balloons while Erin drew barns, haystacks, and fences on each one with colored Magic Markers.

A few counselors arrived to help set up the punch, cake, and party snacks.

"This place looks fabulous, you guys!" Carolyn, the cabin six counselor, told the girls. "You've definitely outdone yourselves."

"We can't take all the credit," Trina reminded her. "The whole camp helped make the animals."

After the last balloon was blown up, Sarah plopped down in a chair. "I'm beat." She sighed. "How much time do we have before everyone starts coming?"

Carolyn looked at her watch. "About five minutes. Oh, I almost forgot. Since you all were hard at work, I picked up your mail for you." She reached into her back pocket.

Carolyn handed Erin a postcard. "Great! My parents are in Switzerland. Maybe they'll buy me a new watch."

Megan was next. "It's a letter from my friend Krista back home."

"Oh, no. Mine's from my twin brothers," Katie said as she ripped open her envelope and pulled out a letter. "It just says, 'Having a wonderful time. Glad you aren't here.' Har. Har."

"Your sister's letter arrived right on schedule, Sarah," Carolyn said. Sarah took the envelope from her counselor but decided not to read it until after the party.

"What about Trina?" Sarah asked and immediately wished she hadn't.

"I'm afraid that's all there is this time," Carolyn apologized.

9

Trina's forehead wrinkled. "Gosh, it's been almost a week and I haven't heard from my mom or dad."

Katie put her arm around her best friend. "I'm sure there's a really good reason for it."

"Didn't you say your father's on a business trip in Japan?" Sarah said.

Trina nodded. "He's been there almost a week."

"Even if he mailed a postcard the first day he got there, it probably wouldn't have gotten here by now," Erin explained authoritatively. Getting postcards from overseas was definitely an area of expertise for Erin, but her reassurances didn't seem to do much to cheer Trina.

Sarah felt sorry for her. This was the first summer Trina had been away from home since her parents' divorce, and Sarah knew Trina counted on their letters more than ever. Up until that day, her parents hadn't let her down; she got a letter from each of them every week. But that week they had disappointed Trina. It was painful for Sarah to watch her try to be cheerful during the festivities.

About a half hour later, all the campers, counselors, and Ms. Winkle were mingling in the dining hall. "There's Deedee!" Megan shouted. "Let's go talk to her." They pushed their way through the crowd. Deedee was surrounded by eight year olds.

Deedee's face lit up when she saw the cabin six girls. "I hear all of these fabulous decorations were your idea. You guys are really super. Thanks," she said.

"Have you heard anything about the new counselor?" Katie asked.

"Ms. Winkle hasn't found anyone yet," Deedee explained. Sarah grinned. "Don't look so happy, Sarah," she teased. "They'll find someone, and it may not be someone who'll cut you as much slack as I do."

Sarah hadn't considered that possibility before. The only thing she looked forward to in archery class was the fact that Deedee always let her get away with a little more than she was supposed to.

Sarah began to worry. What if Deedee's right? she wondered. What if the new person's a cruel archery counselor who forces me to do all the warm-up laps and demands perfect form?

It was not a pleasant thought.

* * *

"Ready for breakfast, guys?" Carolyn asked as she stepped out of her room into the center of the cabin the following Tuesday.

"I'm always ready for blueberry pancakes." Sarah grinned.

"Well, I'm not." Erin sounded exasperated. "The hot water handle in the shower is broken again. I had to wash my hair in the sink. It took so long that now my hair's not dry."

"Erin, let's go. Nobody's going to see you except for a bunch of girls," Katie reminded her, opening the cabin door.

Erin gave her an icy stare. "If I don't dry it properly before I go out, it'll look bad all day. Some people like to look good no matter who's around."

"I'll have Teddy come by to fix the shower," Carolyn said. "But you can't dry your hair now. Ms. Winkle has a big announcement this morning that I'm sure all of you will want to hear."

The girls looked at one another. Ms. Winkle always had announcements to make at meals, but they were generally pretty standard ones like who had won the cleanest cabin award for the week or which cabins had the most intracamp competition points. Never anything to get too excited about.

"What kind of announcement?" Megan asked.

"You'll find out as soon as you put your shoes on and we get over to the dining hall."

"I love surprises!" Megan headed toward the open door.

"Don't get too excited," Katie said. "It's probably just about who the new counselor's going to be."

Sarah's heart practically stopped beating and her stomach started doing somersaults. Ever since the night of Deedee's party, Sarah had sort of been hoping they wouldn't get a new counselor for a while. Now her only hope was that the new counselor would be just as easy as Deedee.

"What's wrong, Sarah?" Trina asked. "You look like you've just seen a ghost."

"No—but maybe a monster," Sarah said.

"What?" Trina sounded puzzled.

"Never mind."

"Well, I don't know about you guys, but if I don't get to the dining hall soon, I'll pass out," Carolyn said. "Let's go."

As usual, the voices of boisterous campers

filled the dining hall. A few girls milled about with plates of pancakes and glasses filled with orange juice while others sat at the long tables eating their breakfasts.

Finally, the camp director stood up to make her announcements. "Please, girls, quiet down." Gradually, each table stopped talking. "Yesterday, I received a call from someone interested in the counselor vacancy. I'm pleased to say that we've decided she'll be a perfect addition to the Sunnyside experience. And I know you girls will just love her. The best part is that she'll be teaching a class in physical fitness."

Sarah looked at her cabin mates. "Physical fitness!" She groaned. "Now I'm sorry I ever complained about archery. At least that didn't require a lot of running and exercising."

"I think a regular physical fitness class might be just what my tennis game needs," Megan commented, her bright red curls bouncing.

"You're just thinking about the bad part of physical fitness," Trina reminded Sarah. "In addition to the running and stuff, we'll probably also play really fun games—like crab soccer."

"Crab soccer is fun? Maybe if you're a contortionist who likes scrambling for an oversized ball on your back," Sarah said.

"The idea is to crawl upside down *without* actually lying on your back," Katie explained.

"I know the object," Sarah began. "I'm just not a big fan of the game."

"For once, I'm on Sarah's side," Erin said. "Physical fitness, ugh."

Unfortunately, Ms. Winkle hadn't mentioned when the new counselor would start. Sarah needed as much time as possible to figure out how to get out of class.

"I wonder what she'll be like," Megan said as they walked back to the cabin together after breakfast.

"I don't have to wonder," Sarah quickly responded. "Anyone who would teach physical fitness *must* be a tyrant."

Trina looked sympathetically at Sarah. "I know you're not really excited about this, Sarah, but we've all got to give her a fair chance. Remember when Carolyn first became the cabin six counselor?"

Sarah smiled, thinking back to the first day of summer camp. None of the girls had been pleased by the thought of a newcomer intruding on the cabin six gang, but it didn't take Carolyn long to fit right in.

"Okay, I'll give her a chance, but I know I'll *never* like physical fitness."

Chapter 2

The following morning, Sarah awoke to a loud knock on the cabin door.

"Oh, I'll get it," Carolyn called as she raced out of her little room.

Sarah rubbed her eyes and searched for her glasses, which were never far from her side. She couldn't see a thing without them. But who would be coming by so early?

"I think I know who it is," Carolyn sang, opening the door wide.

By then, Sarah had found her glasses, and she couldn't believe whom she saw. She was wide awake and jumped down off her bunk. "Alison!" she gasped. Had she actually woken up or was Sarah just dreaming that her sister was only ten feet away? She certainly seemed like the real Alison with her shoulder-length

17

brown hair and round blue eyes surrounded by nearly inch-long lashes.

"What . . . what . . . what are you doing here?" Sarah finally asked.

Alison laughed. "Doesn't a big sister even get a hug?" Sarah stumbled over a tennis shoe as she approached Alison. "Caught you off guard, didn't I?"

"That's the biggest understatement of the year!" Sarah said as she put her arms around her sister. "You haven't told me what you're doing here yet."

"Oh, I got tired of hanging out with Dad all the time," Alison told Sarah.

"Why didn't you tell me you were coming?"

"I wanted to surprise you."

"Well, I think you definitely did that." Carolyn laughed. "You're going to eat breakfast with cabin six, aren't you?"

"You bet. I want to spend as much time with my sister as I can," Alison replied.

"When did you decide to come visit? Will you be staying through dinner?" Sarah rapidly fired off the questions.

"Oh, yes," Alison said. "I'll definitely be staying through dinner." Sarah didn't have a chance to ask more before the others jumped in.

Erin stared at the necklace with the large silver pendant hanging around Alison's neck. "That's really neat," she commented. "Where'd you get it?"

"You have *got* to be Erin," Alison said. She touched the chunk of mishapen silver. "I made it. It was simple. I'll show you how sometime."

"I don't know if there will be time for that," Sarah pointed out.

"Don't worry," Alison said reassuringly. "There'll be plenty of time for us to spend together, too."

Trina stuck out her hand.

"Hi, I'm—" she began.

"Trina," Alison interrupted. "I know. Sarah has told me all about you in her letters. I feel like I've been here at camp with you for the past three years." Alison looked at Megan. "How's your backhand?" she asked.

Megan's mouth dropped open in surprise. "It's my biggest weakness."

Alison leaned close to Megan. "If you promise not to tell Stewart, I'll let you in on my secret to a perfect backhand. It gets 'em every time," she whispered.

"It's a deal." Megan grinned.

"And Katie, I can't wait to meet Starfire," Alison said to the only girl she hadn't met. "Sarah says she's your favorite horse."

"She's the best horse here," Katie said.

"You guys better get ready for breakfast," Carolyn reminded them.

Sarah tore through her belongings looking for a clean pair of shorts and a tee shirt. She wanted to spend every possible minute of the day with her sister before she had to leave.

"Come on, Alison," Sarah said, dragging her sister through the dining hall. "I'll show you which food is safe. I don't want you to spend the day in the infirmary."

"Thanks, Sarah, but if it's okay with you I want to talk to Carolyn alone a second," Alison said. "I'll meet you back at the table in a little while." Sarah was puzzled. Alison had never even met Carolyn until that morning. What could she possibly have to discuss with her that Sarah couldn't hear?

"But—" Sarah started to protest.

"Thanks a lot, Sarah," Alison said and walked off with the counselor.

As she went through the serving line, Sarah kept her eye on Alison and Carolyn. Alison moved her hands wildly and her head bobbed up and down as they talked. Whatever they were talking about couldn't have been too secret since they seemed to be talking in normal tones. But Sarah couldn't understand why Alison had rushed off so suddenly and wished that she could overhear what they were saying.

After they sat down with their trays of food, the cabin six girls had some time to talk among themselves before Carolyn and Alison arrived with their breakfasts.

"You're so lucky you've got an older sister," Katie told Sarah. "Older brothers are the worst, and I got stuck with two of them. If they came for a surprise visit, it would be to surprise me with bugs or snakes or something."

Everyone giggled. Sarah imagined Katie's twin brothers showing up at the cabin door with a bucketful of bugs and laughed even harder. She was so happy that Alison had surprised her with a visit that everything seemed twice as funny.

They talked a little more about how nice it

21

was that Alison decided to visit Sarah and about how cool Alison seemed. Even Erin was impressed. "If I were you, Sarah, I'd pay attention to Alison's great sense of style. You could really learn a lot. Maybe while she's here, we could come up with a new hairstyle for you."

Sarah looked at Alison, who was approaching the table with her tray. She had to agree with Erin. Alison did have great fashion sense. But she looked good in just about anything—even the simple crew neck tee shirt and cuffed blue jean cutoffs she was wearing. Sarah figured it was probably the hand-woven belt that clinched the outfit, though.

Alison looked at the empty chair next to her sister. "I don't want to break cabin six up," she said politely. "If one of you wants to sit next to Sarah, I can pull a chair up to the end of the table."

"We thought you'd probably want to sit next to Sarah since you haven't seen her for so long," Trina explained.

As all the girls chattered about Camp Sunnyside and what activities they did and didn't like, Alison told Sarah about the long hours their father had been working since he'd been elected president of the county physicians' committee.

Alison turned to Carolyn. "Sarah told me you go to State. What are you studying?" she asked.

Carolyn rolled her eyes. "It's pretty dull. Engineering."

Alison laughed. "You don't have to tell me how dull it is," she said. "That's my major, too."

"I don't know if I'll ever go to college." Megan jumped into the conversation. "We had a tennis match at Landview University once, and it was gigantic. I'd probably get lost all the time if I went there."

"With all the tennis scholarships you'll be offered, I'm sure you'll be able to choose a college that's the right size for you," Alison assured her. Megan beamed from the compliment.

"We should take Alison on a Sunnyside tour," Trina suggested. "We can show her all the neat things that are here now, and she can tell us what it was like when she went here."

"Maybe we should canoe over to Eagle and

introduce her to some of the counselors," Erin suggested.

Katie plunked Erin with a spoon. "Give me a break. If you ask me, the farther we are from most of those guys, the better," she said.

"But not *all* of them, huh, Katie?" Alison said inquisitively.

Trina pointed to Katie. "Look, she's turning red," she teased. In all the time Sarah had known her, Katie had practically never blushed. But there was one guy at Eagle she liked to hang out with, Justin. They'd gotten to be good friends when they built a dollhouse together.

"Aww! Ka-tie," Megan and Sarah said in unison.

Erin crossed her arms and shook her head. "You guys are being really childish," she said.

Sarah looked at her older sister, laughing. "You're right," she said. "And we're having tons of fun doing it."

Everyone was having a great time, and Sarah felt really proud that it was mostly due to Alison's surprise visit.

Sarah's thoughts were interrupted when Ms. Winkle stood up and asked everyone to be quiet for the announcements. "I know you girls are all very eager to meet your new counselor," the camp director began.

With the excitement of her sister's visit, Sarah had forgotten all about the new counselor. Sarah looked around, trying to spot the new face in the crowded dining hall.

"The new addition to our staff knows the camp *very* well. She was a Sunnyside camper herself not too long ago. Now I'm pleased to introduce our new camp counselor and physical fitness instructor . . . Alison Fine. Please stand up, Alison, so everyone can meet you," Ms. Winkle instructed.

A loud squeal went up from the cabin six girls as the other campers twisted in their seats to get a glimpse of the new counselor. Sarah could hardly believe she'd heard right. Had Alison really come to live at the camp for the rest of the summer?

Finally, the noise died down. "I hope you'll show her that the Sunnyside spirit is still as strong as ever. Let's welcome her with the camp song."

Everyone—including Alison—joined in as Ms. Winkle belted out,

"I'm a Sunnyside girl, with a Sunnyside
smile,
And I spend my summers in Sunnyside style,
I have sunny, sunny times with my Sunny-
side friends,
And I know I'll be sad when the summer
ends,
But I'll always remember, with joy and pride,
My sunny, sunny days at Sunnyside!"

A loud cheer filled the room.

Alison turned to her sister. "After I got your
letter about the position that opened here, I
called Ms. Winkle," she said, a smile filling
up her face. "I don't know why I didn't think
of it before. I'm gone all year at college, and
then you leave for camp almost as soon as I
get home for the summer. We hardly ever get
to see each other—until now. I wanted it to be
a surprise, so I asked Ms. Winkle not to mention it to you. I hope you're not mad."

"Are you kidding? This is going to be great.
We've never been Sunnyside campers *together* before." Sarah smiled. "We're going to
have tons of fun, and Dad won't be around
to tell us to quiet down—"

"Or help with the laundry—"

"Or eat all our broccoli!" The two sisters burst into laughter. The day had hardly begun and already it was the best day at camp Sarah had ever had.

That afternoon, Alison had to meet with Ms. Winkle and the other counselors and plan her physical fitness class, so Sarah spent the afternoon without her.

"Why don't we all do something together today during free time?" Trina suggested.

"Sure," Sarah agreed. "How about swimming?"

"Count me in," Erin said. "I need to work on my tan."

Sarah liked swimming and she usually spent every possible minute in the water. But that morning's news had really taken her by surprise, so while Megan, Katie, and Trina played a particularly raucous game of Shark, Sarah sat on the pool platform preoccupied with her thoughts.

The idea that Alison was there to stay for the summer had finally sunk in. Of course, Sarah was happy to see her sister and thought it was great that everyone seemed to like Alison immediately. But the initial excitement had worn off a little, and now Sarah sort of wished she'd had more time to adjust to the idea before Alison actually showed up at the cabin door.

Erin sat on the blanket next to Sarah, smoothing suntan lotion and baby oil on her body. Suddenly, chilly water drops pelted both girls.

"Hey!" Erin screeched, jumping up from her spot on the blanket. "Be careful where you splash!"

"Sorry." Megan giggled. "You guys should come in. We could use a couple more people."

"No, thank you," Erin told Megan. "Water games are so babyish. Right, Sarah?"

Sarah had been only partly conscious of the activity around her. "Huh? . . . Oh, yeah." She nodded, not even looking up.

As Erin went to find something to dry off with, Megan pushed herself up on the side of the pool and sat on the blanket next to Sarah. "What's wrong?" Megan asked.

Sarah should have figured her best friend would pick up on her mood and begin to worry. She also should have figured Megan wouldn't be convinced when she said, "Nothing."

Megan shook her head so that her wet curls bounced around her shoulders. "This is practically the first time we've been able to get out of the cabin for almost a week and you haven't even put your toe in the water yet. Something's *got* to be wrong."

Sarah considered making things easier on herself by telling Megan she couldn't go swimming because she had her period. But Sarah didn't want to lie to her friend. "Well . . ." Sarah hesitated, hoping her words wouldn't come out all wrong, "I guess I'm a little worried about having Alison here at camp."

"You were so excited when you found out she was the new counselor. What are you worried about?" Megan asked. "Alison's great. Besides, you're always talking about how much you miss her."

"I do miss her, and I'm really glad she found a new job so quickly. But . . . I miss her at *home.*" Megan looked almost as confused as Sarah felt. The words weren't coming out the way she'd wanted them to. How could she explain the feeling of independence she had at Sunnyside? "We get along real well but sometimes we have problems because she

29

thinks of me as her *baby* sister. But my dad's always around to mediate any problems between us at home."

"I don't think you need to worry about that, Sarah," Megan comforted her. "There's no time for fighting here. Besides, you've got us to stick up for you."

Sarah hung her head and couldn't help noticing her belly sticking out a little. "I guess so. But I sure didn't expect Alison to be the physical fitness instructor."

"You're thinking about all the bad stuff, Sarah. Maybe Alison's being the new counselor is the best thing for you. Think about it. You wanted someone who would give you as many breaks as Deedee did. Alison will probably be an even bigger pushover. You've got it made. Now you won't have to do archery *or* physical fitness." Megan smiled mischievously.

Sarah perked up. "You're probably right," she said. "I never thought of it that way."

Sarah got up off her blanket, stepped to the edge of the pool, and jumped into the water.

Chapter 3

Sarah didn't see Alison again until the next day at lunch. It had started to rain again the night before, so she had spent most of the evening on her bunk reading her novel, which she was eager to finish before she bought the sequel on the next trip to Pine Ridge.

The cabin six girls were gathered around a table eating that day's main course, macaroni and cheese, when Alison approached them.

"Mind if I sit here?" Alison asked. "I don't want to interrupt anything."

"Sure." Sarah smiled, motioning toward the chair directly in front of her. "We weren't really talking about anything important."

"Well, I can't stay long anyway," Alison explained to her sister. "I just wanted to make sure you're okay and apologize for not being able to spend too much time with you."

"That's all right. I figured you were hunched over nutrition books and fitness manuals discovering cruel and unusual methods of torture." Sarah giggled.

Alison smiled. "Are you kidding? Dad would never forgive me if I hurt his baby."

Sarah looked over at the others, and Megan gave her a knowing wink. Sarah knew her cabin mates wouldn't mind if Alison let her off a little easy, but she wasn't sure it was such a good idea for Alison to be so obvious about her intentions.

Alison pushed her chair away from the table and picked up her tray. "Well, I better go," Alison excused herself. "I have to ask Ms. Winkle a question before lunch is over." Before she walked away, she bent over Erin, who had been sitting next to her. "That's a really beautiful barrette."

Erin beamed at the compliment. "Thanks. My parents got it for me in France last summer."

As Alison walked away, Erin leaned toward the center of the table and whispered, "Gosh, I always thought being an only child was the greatest. But now I see how lucky you are, Sarah. Alison's really great—and she's got fabulous taste."

"Believe me," Katie said skeptically, "not all siblings are like Alison. She's just really cool—because she's *not* an older brother."

"She's not twins, either." Megan laughed.

"Yeah, it's kind of strange that you two are so different," Erin commented.

Sarah wasn't sure how to take the remark, but she didn't worry about it. She was wondering about Trina, who was off in another world—and the look on her face convinced Sarah that it was a pretty sad one.

"Are you okay, Trina?" Sarah asked.

"Huh? . . . Oh, yes, I'm fine," Trina said. "I was . . . I was just thinking about how much fun physical fitness class will be." Sarah knew that whatever Trina was thinking about, it wasn't anything fun, but she didn't want to push her friend. Trina would talk about her problems when and if she was ready.

"Speaking of physical fitness, I have to go back to the cabin to get something I'll need for class," Sarah said. "I'll meet you guys there."

She walked along the path back to the

cabin, opened the door, and grabbed her book off the bunk. She needed something to read so she wouldn't be bored when Alison let her take it easy in class.

Megan, Trina, Katie, and Erin were talking with Brandy and Melissa from cabin seven when Sarah arrived at the activities hall. Gymnastics mats were spread out over the floor. Two other girls from cabin seven were turning cartwheels and doing back flips while a couple others sat in a corner talking.

Just as Sarah walked over to where her friends were gathered, Alison stepped through the open door.

Everyone stopped what she was doing and stared. Alison had a whistle around her neck and a clipboard in one hand. "Welcome to physical fitness training. Since I'm the new one here at Sunnyside, I'll need to play catch-up for a while. So to start out, everyone have a seat on the mats. I'd like to hear a little bit about each of you."

Sarah could tell that the cabin seven girls were pretty impressed by Alison. A couple of them looked at each other and nodded.

Megan introduced herself first. "Well, I like

sports, but I really love tennis. I hope that someday I'll play at Wimbledon—and win!''

One of the cabin seven girls went next. "My name is Kathy, and I'm from Kirkwood. I like art and horseback riding."

"It's nice to meet you," Alison answered. "Those were my two favorite activities when I was your age, too."

Everyone else followed, talking about where they were from and what activities they liked best. Alison always had something nice to say when each girl finished and looked especially impressed when Trina and Brandy said they were counselors-in-training for some of the nine year olds.

Finally, everyone had introduced herself except Sarah. "Sarah, why don't you say a little bit about yourself?" Alison asked. Sarah was a little surprised at first—so were the other cabin six girls. What could Sarah possibly tell Alison that she didn't already know? Their mother had died when Sarah was only three, so Alison had been her substitute mother in a lot of ways.

I bet Alison doesn't want to make it too obvious that I'm her sister so she can give me breaks, Sarah thought. That way, when she's easy on me, no one else will know why. Sarah decided to wait until later to let Alison know that word spread fast and most of the girls at Sunnyside already knew they were related.

Sarah tried to look serious. "Well, this is my third year at Sunnyside," she began. "My hobbies are reading and writing. And I have an older sister." Sarah couldn't keep a straight face any longer and laughed out loud at her own joke. Samantha and Liza from cabin seven joined in.

Alison ignored the laughter and continued class. "Thanks, girls. Normally we'll meet outside on the field, but on rainy or muddy days like today, just come directly to the activities hall," Alison explained. "There are plenty of effective aerobic and stretching exercises to do indoors. And I even have some ideas for indoor games." She got up.

"Now please line up in four straight columns so we can begin calisthenics." Sarah picked up her book and stood behind Megan. Katie, Melissa, and Kathy took the other front spots.

Alison eyed her sister knowingly. "Sarah . . . I'll just keep your book up here until we're finished for the day," she offered, holding out her hand. Sarah handed the book over to her sister hesitantly. At first, she was a little annoyed, but Sarah reminded herself that in order for Alison's new position to work to her advantage, the favoritism couldn't be too obvious.

Alison spread her feet about two feet apart on the mat. "Stretching exercises build greater flexibility to help you move more easily," she explained, spreading her feet a little more and placing her left hand near her left knee. "Slowly lean to one side like this and hold your position for ten seconds. Don't bounce," she warned.

Most of the girls from cabin six and seven followed Alison's lead. Sarah noticed that Erin wasn't making much of an effort. She also noticed Alison watching Erin.

"The wonderful thing about the exercises we'll be doing is that they're great for your figure," Alison began. "Each one works on a specific set of muscles, but you'll have allover muscle tone. Plus, you're burning calories. With relatively little effort every day, you won't have to worry about unattractive bulges and bumps for a lifetime."

Sarah had seen Alison in action enough

times to know what she was up to. But Erin didn't, and Alison's psychology worked wonders on her. Erin began stretching and straining her leg muscles. Sarah had never seen Erin work so hard at anything athletic.

The girls around Sarah looked like they were having an easy time with the first exercise, but she could feel a painful burning in her thigh after only a couple of minutes. As the group moved on to more difficult stretches, Sarah didn't lean as hard.

The sitting stretches were even more difficult for Sarah. Alison had the girls alternate between their right and left legs and then stretch straight out in front.

While Trina and Erin bent all the way to the mat, Sarah couldn't lean more than a couple inches. The burning started again, this time in a different part of her legs.

Sarah looked around the room to see if everyone was having as much trouble as she was. Even if they couldn't touch their heads to the mat, most of the girls could go at least halfway. Sarah tried to push herself a little farther, but the pain became unbearable.

Luckily, Alison saved her. "Okay, that's enough stretching." She smiled at the room.

"Take a five-minute break. Then, we'll play a game of dodge ball. Cabin six versus cabin seven."

Sarah was grateful for the chance to rest and sat with her legs crossed on the mat. She wanted to spend the break reading her book, but she couldn't even muster the strength to get up and get it.

Trina, Brandy, and Megan circled around Alison while some of the girls talked to each other or continued to practice some of the stretching exercises. The activity seemed to go on for only a minute or two before Alison shouted that it was time to start again.

Sarah lethargically pushed herself off the mat while the other girls quickly moved to one side of the room or the other.

Alison pointed to a crack in the mats. "This will be the dividing line," she explained. "Does everyone know the rules?" When all the girls nodded, Alison tossed the ball up in the air between the teams. Players from both sides scrambled to throw the first out.

Sarah maneuvered out of the way of the racing ball. She felt triumphant when she managed to send one of the slower cabin seven girls out of the game. She looked at Alison,

39

expecting congratulations, but Alison was too busy shouting, "Nice try, Trina" and "Maybe next time, Kathy."

Sarah was proud of her great play, but the chances of her getting another of the girls out before someone got her was a long shot. She found a safe corner of the court where the ball rarely went. All she had to do was stand out of the way, and she'd probably be safe.

Sarah's mind began to drift to the world of *Through the Crystal Mirror*. What if all I had to do to get out of physical fitness class was step through a mirror? she wondered.

Her eyes fell on the cover of the novel lying on the floor at the front of the room. She began to imagine that she was the novel's heroine, the wisest person in the kingdom of Zorbock, whom everyone looked up to. She wondered if she would choose the fantasy world through the mirror or the real world with friends and parents.

Suddenly, the ball hit Sarah right on the thigh and interrupted her thoughts. "Okay, everyone can stop now. Cabin seven wins." Sarah had been so far away in her thoughts, she hadn't noticed that she was the last one left on her team.

Alison had noticed. But instead of being impressed that Sarah had lasted so long, she said, "Sarah, you hardly tried at all. You just stood in the corner and let your teammates do all the work to protect you. I don't think that's really fair."

Sarah looked around the room at all the faces that had turned to stare at her. "Oh, come on, Alison. I almost won the game for us." Sarah grinned smugly and crossed her arms.

Alison sighed and leaned toward Sarah. "While we're in class, you should talk to me the way you would any other counselor," she said quietly. Before Sarah had a chance to defend herself, Alison turned to the other girls. "Okay, you can go enjoy free time. That was a great first day. Congratulations, cabin seven."

Sarah couldn't look at her sister. How could Alison treat her that way in front of everyone? Sarah's only consolation was that she knew her cabin mates would think Alison was too tough on her, but that didn't excuse Alison. And it didn't erase the embarrassment she was feeling.

Sarah scooped up her book and headed out

the door of the hall. Erin was the first one out, and Alison didn't say anything to her, she thought. And Trina and Megan weren't really working hard either. It comes naturally to them.

As Sarah sulked back to the cabin, she heard her friends talking excitedly behind her. She slowed down a little, waiting to hear what they had to say about Alison now. "Those stretching exercises were great!" Megan said. "Alison said that we'll work on cardiovascular exercises next time. By the end of the summer, I'll be able to take Stewart on with one arm tied behind my back."

"I hope it's not the arm you serve with," Katie joked, and the other girls laughed.

Sarah couldn't understand why Alison had humiliated her when she knew how much she hated sports. But what was even tougher to figure out was why her friends weren't consoling her—and why they seemed to like the class and Alison even after they'd seen what she'd done to Sarah.

Chapter 4

Sarah was climbing onto her bunk as her friends walked into the cabin. She fluffed her pillow and opened her book.

"Why don't you come watch me cream Stewart?" Megan asked. "I feel like today's my lucky day."

"No, thanks. My legs hurt pretty bad," Sarah complained without looking up. "I'd rather just stay here and read."

"You can bring your book to the tennis courts," Megan suggested. "And I promise we won't make you chase any balls."

"I just want to be alone for a while," Sarah snapped. When she saw Megan's smile fade, she immediately felt bad. After all, Megan was just trying to help. It wasn't her fault that Ms. Winkle had hired Alison to be a Sun-

43

nyside counselor. In a gentler voice Sarah said, "I'm nearly finished with my book. If I don't stay inside, I probably won't finish."

"All right," Megan said, cheering up a little. "But if you change your mind, you know where to find me."

Everyone except Sarah changed clothes and headed through the cabin door for free time. Erin was the last to leave since she had to shampoo and dry her hair.

After Erin was gone, Sarah tried to concentrate on her novel. She flipped from side to side and turned upside down so that her head was at the foot of the bed. She even moved to Megan's bottom bunk. Nothing worked. Sarah had to read much slower than usual for anything to sink in. She even had to reread a few pages.

Sarah couldn't forget about the way that Alison had spoken to her. But why had she taken her anger at Alison out on Megan? It wasn't Megan's fault she was athletic. Then again, even someone who loved sports should have noticed that Alison had been really harsh with Sarah.

It was no use. Sarah couldn't get through a single page without thinking about how awful her afternoon—and the rest of the summer—were going to be.

After what seemed like an eternity of loneliness, Trina and Katie flew through the door, laughing and breathing hard. Sarah looked up and smiled.

"You never told us what a horse nut Alison is," Katie said.

Sarah's smile drooped. She would rather spend the whole day by herself than hear more talk about Alison.

Katie peeked over Sarah's shoulder. "What were you doing while we were gone?" she asked. "You should have finished that book by now."

"Oh, yeah. Well, you know how it is with a good fantasy. You sort of get carried away with your own daydreams."

Trina shook her head. "I think you better leave the daydreaming to Megan," she teased. "One overdeveloped imagination in the cabin is enough."

Sarah joined in the laughter. She was glad to be talking about something other than Alison. But it didn't last.

"I really liked Alison's riding pants," Trina

told Katie. "I'm going to save my baby-sitting money this fall and buy a pair."

"I'm not waiting until then. I'm using my allowance and getting a pair at the Jolly Equestrian on our next trip to Pine Ridge."

"I'll help you pick a pair out. I need to get a book, so I'm definitely going next time," Sarah interrupted, hoping she could turn the conversation to something other than Alison.

Katie missed the hint completely and continued talking about her new favorite subject. "Didn't Alison look great on Starfire?" she asked.

Sarah looked at Katie in amazement. Katie always made sure she got to ride her favorite horse. Sarah was sure she must have misunderstood. "You let Alison ride Starfire?" she asked.

"Sure. Don't look so shocked," Katie said. "I'm not the only person here who can ride Starfire."

"It's just that everyone else knows that when you're around, they should let you have Starfire," Sarah explained. "I'm surprised you let Alison take her like that."

"She didn't take her; I asked her to ride Starfire," Katie said.

"You asked someone else to ride Starfire? Which horse did you ride?" Sarah asked.

"Bess." Sarah's mouth dropped open as she gasped. Bess was the slowest horse at Sunnyside. Katie usually laughed at the girls who got stuck with Bess. She was always the last horse chosen—except when Sarah was riding. Bess was the only horse slow enough to make Sarah feel comfortable.

"Alison says that she can remember when Bess was the fastest horse at Sunnyside," Trina explained.

Katie continued to explain to no one in particular that nobody really gave Bess a chance. "You can tell what a superior horse she once was," she said. "And even now, with the proper rider, I bet she'd be almost as fast as Starfire."

While Katie went on, Trina sat down on her bunk and put her elbows on her knees and her chin in her hands. Sarah gazed at her in concern. Just moments before, Trina had been in such a good mood. Katie noticed that too.

"Trina? Are you okay?"

Trina looked up. "Oh, sorry. I was just thinking about how great it must be to have someone like Alison around all the time who can tell you stories and expose you to all kinds of great things."

"Yeah, it's nice, but I don't get to see her much anymore," Sarah reminded her.

Trina fidgeted with the hem of her shorts. "It's just that it's always been weird being the only kid around the house. Sometimes it gets kind of lonely. I just think that maybe if I'd had a sister like Alison, the divorce might have been a little easier."

Sarah thought about her own home. Even though she couldn't remember when her mother died, she knew it had really helped to have Alison around.

Like the time Sarah wanted to be in the Daisies, one of the most popular groups of girls at school. To become an official member, Sarah was supposed to tell the principal that Leonard Thigpen, the smartest and most repulsive kid in school, had cheated on his science test.

Sarah really wanted to be a Daisy. But even though she hadn't liked Leonard ever since he put ketchup in her milk, she didn't want to lie about him. Alison had helped her understand that it was more important to be honest to herself and others than it was to be in the "right" group.

At that moment, Erin stormed into the cabin yelling, "Why me?" and ran into the bathroom. Sarah, Katie, and Trina exchanged perplexed glances.

Megan bounced in the door behind Erin. "What's up?" she asked.

Erin peeked around the corner. "I've got a rash! On my face!" she wailed.

Sarah was relieved that it wasn't something more serious. She couldn't believe that Erin was making such a big deal out of a little rash, though.

Katie rolled her eyes. "I knew all that gunk that you put on your face couldn't be good for you," she said, slipping on her Walkman earphones.

Sarah was more sympathetic. She admired Erin for being able to wear makeup without being self-conscious. She'd tried it once, too, but it just didn't fit her personality. "Maybe you overdid it with one of your moisturizers," she suggested.

"I'm sure it's just this horrible soap. I ran out of the supply my mother sent me, so I had to use the crummy stuff they give out here.

My skin is *much* too delicate," Erin explained.

"Look on the bright side," Megan suggested. "Now you don't have to worry about the chlorine in the pool ruining your hair. Darrell probably won't let you swim with a rash."

"Yeah, and the only activity we have planned with Eagle is a camp fire," Sarah added. "It'll be too dark for Bobby to see anything."

"The object is not for him to see nothing," Erin stated. "The object is for him to appreciate how beautiful I am." She gave her cabin mates a disgusted look. "Maybe you'll understand someday."

They ignored Erin as she went into the bathroom. "Oh—Sarah, thanks for reminding me," Megan said.

"About what?" Sarah asked, sitting on the edge of her bunk.

"I ran into Alison on my way back from my tennis game," Megan began.

"Did you beat Stewart?" Sarah interrupted, trying again to keep the conversation from focusing on her older sister.

"No, but I won all six games in the second

set. Anyway, Alison told me that she convinced Ms. Winkle to let us play records at the camp fire."

Katie yanked her earphones off her head. *"Real* music?" Katie asked. "We've been trying to get her to let us play records all summer."

Erin walked into the main room with a sloppy green mask smeared over her face. "What's all the excitement?"

Katie told Erin the news. "No more babyish camp fire songs?" Erin asked.

"Well, I wouldn't go that far—yet," Megan told her. "Besides, I like most of the songs we sing. But I also like it when someone else is doing the singing."

Katie tossed back her head and pretended to be playing a guitar. "And making the music."

Picking up the cue, Erin jumped on her bed. She held her hand as if there was a microphone in it and whipped her blond braid around in the air as she sang, " 'I can't get over losing you. Girl, whatcha done to me. Girl, you make me cra-zy!' "

"Aaah!" Megan shrieked, pretending to faint on the cabin floor.

Sarah didn't come down from her bunk, but as the girls all began to laugh, Sarah's mood lightened. Maybe she was overreacting. Alison was still a good sister, and once she settled into the Camp Sunnyside routine a little more, she probably wouldn't be so uptight.

Chapter 5

Sarah could barely keep up with Darrell's commands the next morning in swimming class. Every time she kicked her legs, she felt like weights were attached to her feet.

"What's wrong?" Darrell asked as Sarah struggled up the pool ladder.

"I guess I'm worn out from yesterday," she explained.

"I heard your sister really gave you a workout. Why don't you take it a little easy today? It's dangerous to swim when you're tired."

Sarah wasn't thrilled that she had to miss out on her favorite class because of physical fitness. But Darrell was right. Sarah was having trouble keeping her head above water, and she decided to watch the other girls from the sidelines a while.

53

Just as she found an out-of-the-way spot on the edge of the pool, Alison appeared. "Can I join you?" She smiled.

"I don't mind," Sarah answered, "if it's okay with Darrell."

The handsome swimming instructor looked down when he heard his name. "You're not being too tough on my sister, are you?" Alison asked him.

"Sarah's my most improved swimmer," he explained. "If anything, she's tough on herself." Sarah noticed the surprised look on Alison's face. Couldn't her sister believe she was capable of anything athletic?

It was true that when she was little, the extent of Sarah's swimming expertise had been holding onto the side of the pool and kicking her feet. But that summer, Sarah had been writing Alison letters all along, telling her about the lifesaving techniques she'd mastered. Obviously, Alison hadn't believed it was possible. Sarah wanted to jump in at that moment and prove it to her sister, but she didn't want to disobey Darrell.

"Hey, Alison," Katie shouted from the diving board as Megan and Trina waved from where they were standing in line. "Watch this." She did a perfect back flip, barely causing a splash.

Alison applauded as Katie surfaced. "Maybe later you can show me how to do that," she said.

Erin got up from her place at the side of the pool. "Why aren't you swimming with the others?" Alison asked as Erin sat down next to her. "I didn't wear you out, too, did I?"

"No, this camp is ruining my skin," Erin complained.

Alison examined Erin's rash, which by then had become redder and had crept from her chin to part of her neck. "I've got something in my cabin that I think will clear that right up. And I'll show you what to use so that doesn't happen again," Alison told her.

"Thanks a lot." Erin smiled.

Alison stood up. "I need to go talk to Carolyn. I'll see you at lunch—and class."

Class came much too soon for Sarah. The second day was even harder than the first had been. Alison didn't spend as much time on the stretches and quickly moved into aerobic exercises. She bounced up and down, alternating right leg kicks with left leg kicks. After the cabin six and seven girls joined in and did that for a while, Alison gradually added arm motions and more complicated steps.

"Great job, Megan and Katie!" Alison shouted between breaths. "Come on, Samantha, you can keep it going! Don't give up now, Liza."

Sarah tried to keep up. She was determined to prove that she was just as capable as her cabin mates. But lifting her legs off the ground became more and more difficult, and she could barely move her arms from her sides. Fifteen minutes into the class, Sarah was out of breath and flat on her back.

From her supine position, Sarah heard her sister say, "Okay, everyone. Take a short break, but try to keep moving. You don't want your muscles to tense up."

Finally, Sarah thought to herself and shut her eyes. But the next thing she knew, Alison was kneeling beside her.

"It's only the second day. Have I worn you out completely?" Alison asked sympathetically.

Sarah was encouraged that Alison actually seemed to care. She opened her eyes. "Yeah. I'm not used to this. The most exercise I get is swimming, and Darrell lets us work at our own speed," Sarah explained.

"All I'm asking is that you work as hard here as you do in swimming class," Alison said.

"I'm surprised you're even acknowledging that I do *that* well," Sarah said, looking her sister directly in the eyes for the first time.

Alison lowered her voice. "Sarah, I asked you not to speak to me that way in class," she said firmly. "Here, I'm your counselor, not your sister." Sarah looked away as Alison said in a louder voice, "I know it hurts, but it won't get easier. You don't want to be old and out of shape, do you?"

"That's better than being young and in pain," Sarah mumbled. Alison looked disappointed with her younger sister. "I'm not asking you to be a superstar athlete overnight," she said. "All I'm asking is for you to try a little harder." Alison pushed herself off the mat and announced, "Break's over! Line up and count off for relay teams."

Sarah got in position with the others and pushed herself to finish the class. Even though Alison had singled her out and been kind of mean, Sarah was thankful that she hadn't publicly humiliated her that time.

After class, Sarah's cabin mates were sympathetic. "Maybe you should take an aspirin," Trina suggested. "It might make the aching go away."

"That's a good idea," Megan agreed. "I'll go with you to see the nurse."

"What she really needs is a professional massage. My parents took me to a masseuse for my birthday," Erin said.

"Thanks, but I think I'll just go and read," Sarah said.

"You know, Sarah," Katie said. "Maybe if you got a little more exercise and read a little less every day, you wouldn't hurt so much when you had to work out a little." The others nodded.

"It's not my fault class is right after lunch," Sarah defended herself. "It's not safe to exercise so soon after eating."

"What about swimming class?" Katie asked. "That's right after breakfast, and you don't mind it."

Sarah put her hands on her hips. "Oh, come on, you guys," she said. "You know that was a tough workout. You may not have been having trouble, but I noticed some of the girls—like Samantha and Liza—were." Sarah grabbed her towel and went into the bathroom to take a shower.

As she washed the sweat and grime off herself, Sarah thought about what Katie had said. She knew her friends were concerned about her. But before Alison came, they talked about how much weight she'd lost and what a great swimmer she'd become. Now they acted as if all she did was lie in bed and eat candy bars.

Sarah was happy to wake up the next morning and see rain coming down in sheets. Alison had said that if they were indoors again, the class would be devoted to testing. She wasn't exactly looking forward to the blood pressure and body fat tests, but at least Sarah's muscles would get a break, and Alison wouldn't be able to accuse her of not working hard enough.

Sarah had gotten over her hurt from the day before. Katie hadn't meant to offend her. It was understandable that the girls would be influenced by Alison. Sarah was sure that by the end of the day the novelty of Alison and the new class would wear off and things would be back to normal in cabin six.

To protect themselves from the rain, the girls had worn blue jeans and sweatshirts for morning activities. So they had to return to the cabin to change into their tee shirts and shorts for physical fitness.

As Sarah dressed, she looked around at her cabin mates. Trina had already finished dressing and sat on the edge of her bed looking distant. Megan was down on her hands and knees saying, "I know that tennis shoe is here somewhere," as Katie and Erin were pulling their hair back in front of the mirror.

Considerate Trina, enthusiastic Megan, energetic Katie, and sophisticated Erin. Who could blame Alison for being disappointed in her after getting to know Sarah's cabin mates? But it wasn't their fault they were naturals at physical fitness, and Sarah wasn't going to hold a grudge.

She bent down to tie her shoe. "When I went for my camp physical, the doctor checked my muscle tone." Sarah smiled. "I can't wait to see how much it's improved now that I've been swimming."

60

"I bet it'll be ten times better," Megan encouraged her.

"Do you think so?" Sarah said smiling. "I guess I do look a lot stronger."

"Are you guys ready?" Katie asked, grabbing her raincoat. The other girls pulled on theirs and dodged the drops as Katie led the way to the activities hall. Sarah knew she wouldn't do as well as the other girls, but at least she'd be able to see how much she'd improved.

"Hi, girls. Did you park your rowboat outside?" Alison joked as they peeled off their jackets.

Sarah smiled weakly at her sister and shook the rain out of her ponytail as her friends said, "Hi." The cabin seven girls were already there. Tables were set up along the walls and a yardstick was taped next to one of them.

Sarah took her spot on the mat so that Alison could take roll. Alison stood up with her clipboard and pen and scanned the group. Her eyes stopped on a girl in the third row.

"Liza, you know you're not supposed to be wearing jeans," Alison reminded one of the cabin seven girls.

"All my shorts were dirty, and I didn't borrow any since we were just doing testing."

"I'm afraid I'm going to have to give you a demerit," Alison said firmly. "You have to come to every class prepared."

At that moment, Sarah got a sinking feeling in her stomach. Oh, no! She had forgotten to put socks on. She tucked her feet under her folded legs and hoped that her sister wouldn't notice.

"I'm also going to have to give you a demerit since you're not wearing socks, Sarah," Alison said.

Sarah's head dropped. "Sorry," she mumbled. Then she had an idea. "I'll go back to the cabin and get a pair."

Alison shook her head. "Since it's pouring rain and we won't be exercising today, that won't be necessary."

Sarah opened her mouth to protest when Alison interrupted her. "Even if I let you go back to the cabin, I'd still have to give you a demerit," she explained. "You know you're supposed to come to class ready."

Sarah stared stonily at her sister. But Alison refused to back down and gave the girls instructions for the testing stations.

Alison wouldn't let a day go by without finding *something* wrong with her younger sister. Sarah moped from station to station, forgetting how excited she'd been before class. She didn't even pay attention when Megan told her the results of their blood pressure tests.

When the girls got back to cabin six, Trina suggested that everyone go to the dining hall for free time. "It's practically stopped raining, so we won't get much wetter than we already are," she said.

"Alison and I were going to go to the arts and crafts cabin to work on the rug I'm weaving," Katie said, "but I can do that tomorrow."

"Why should we waste our time in the dining hall?" Erin asked. "The little kids will be there playing games." The cabin six girls usually just stayed in their cabin on rainy days and read, wrote letters, or played a game of their own.

"Trina's got a good idea," Megan said cheerfully, looking at Sarah. "It might take our minds off . . . um . . . things."

"I better not go. If Alison doesn't like what

I'm wearing, she'll just give me a demerit," Sarah said sarcastically.

"That's not really fair," Trina said. "Alison wouldn't give you a demerit if you weren't doing anything wrong."

Sarah wasn't surprised to hear her cabin mate taking her sister's side. Cabin six girls always stuck together. But it seemed as if each day that Alison had been there, the other girls had gotten closer to her.

Sarah didn't want to argue with Trina, but she had to defend herself. "I wasn't doing anything wrong today," Sarah complained.

"You didn't have any socks on," Katie reminded her.

"I offered to go back and get a pair."

Megan stepped over to Sarah, who was sitting on her bunk with her arms crossed in front of her. "I don't really think you can say Alison is picking on you," Megan said gently. "Other counselors have given you demerits. And Alison has given other girls demerits."

"But I'm not other girls," Sarah complained. "I'm her sister. She knows how bad I am at sports." Sarah felt as if she was going to burst with anger.

"You can't expect Alison to treat you differently just because you're her sister," Katie noted.

"Alison did what any counselor would have done," Trina said. "But there are advantages to her being around that you wouldn't have gotten if Ms. Winkle had picked another counselor. Most of us have to wait for a letter to come before we hear from a relative. You have your sister right here to talk to any time you want."

Sarah didn't want to hear Trina go on again about how lucky Sarah was to have an older sister to talk to. According to Katie, Erin, and Trina, Alison was always right and Sarah was always doing something wrong.

It wasn't fair! Sarah got up and headed out the door.

Chapter 6

Sarah was sorry she'd left the cabin in such a big rush. She'd forgotten to bring her raincoat, and even though the rain had subsided some, it hadn't stopped altogether. Sarah needed to find shelter and peace and quiet fast, and before she knew it she was following a trail into the woods.

She found a tree stump that the huge trees overhead blocked from the raindrops, except for an occasional drip off the leaves.

Even though Sarah knew the woods were strictly off-limits, she made herself comfortable on the stump, dangling her legs so they wouldn't touch the ground. Everyone's in the dining hall for rainy day activities. With the bad weather, they'll just assume I went back to the cabin to read, she thought.

With nothing to do alone in the woods, Sarah began to wish she'd brought her novel along. She had only a couple chapters left and she still had absolutely no idea how the story would end. Had the mirror cracked so badly that Linda could never return home to her family? This was the first book she'd read by Lilly Murdock, but already she couldn't wait to go to Pine Ridge to get the second and third stories in the trilogy.

A snapping twig startled Sarah. When she turned around to see what made the noise, Alison's tall form towered above her. "Are you all right, Sarah?" her older sister asked.

Sarah breathed a sigh of relief and nodded. Although Alison wasn't exactly a welcome sight, Sarah was glad to see that the noise hadn't been made by Ms. Winkle or a wild animal.

"I hope you're not mad at me because of what happened this morning," Alison said, squatting next to Sarah. "Please try to understand that if I want a computer, I can't afford to lose another job," Alison explained.

Sarah stared at her sister. "What's that have to do with me?" she asked curtly.

"Well, nothing *exactly*," Alison said. "But

Ms. Winkle made it very clear to me that if I showed any favoritism to you, I couldn't stay at Sunnyside. They usually don't even hire sisters as counselors, but she made an exception since Sunnyside and I were both so desperate."

"That doesn't mean you have to be so hard on me," Sarah pointed out. "Especially since you're not hard on Trina or the other girls."

"That's not true, Sarah," Alison raised her voice. "I gave one of the other girls a demerit today."

"Not one of the cabin six girls."

"They came to class dressed properly," Alison said, raising her voice slightly.

"Erin's not a very good athlete, and you don't yell at her for not trying," Sarah pointed out.

"Erin may not be very enthusiastic about sports, but she works hard at the exercises and makes an effort during the games."

Sarah could see Alison's point. Before Alison came, Erin had hated most of the athletic activities. But since Alison had made the point about aerobics and muscle tone, Erin had really gone all out in physical fitness class.

"I guess I understand," Sarah said half-heartedly.

"I'm glad." Alison smiled. "Let's go back to the camp." Sarah stood up and followed her sister. They walked a few steps before either spoke again.

"Sarah? There's something else I have to tell you," Alison said.

Sarah didn't look up. The tone of Alison's voice told her she wouldn't like what Alison had to say. "What?" she snapped.

"I'll have to give you a demerit for going into the woods alone," Alison said.

Sarah froze. How underhanded! Alison had just set her up with a nice conversation just so she could pick on her again. Their talk had just been nothing but a manipulation tactic. Alison was on a power trip, and she was really enjoying handing out demerits to her defenseless sister. She'd show her who was defenseless!

Sarah stormed ahead of Alison, tromping right through muddy spots. She didn't care, though. The more she thought about Alison's trick the more furious she became. Sarah wasn't going to fall for her buddy-buddy routine anymore. If Alison wasn't going to try to

70

understand Sarah's position, Sarah didn't want to listen to hers.

Sarah heard Alison call her name, but she didn't turn around. There wasn't enough room at Sunnyside for both Fine sisters. No matter what it took, Sarah would see to it that Alison wouldn't be making a nuisance of herself much longer.

Sarah wanted to get her book, but she couldn't take the chance that the other girls were still in the cabin. She didn't want her cabin mates to gang up on her again. Alison had already abused her enough for a while.

Sarah stood in the drizzle, trying to figure out where to go to get away from her sister and avoid running into her cabin mates. She remembered how upset Liza had looked when Alison had given her the demerit that day.

Sarah had never given Liza much thought before. They'd never really done anything together. Liza was into crafts and games, she was giggly, and Sarah had never seen Liza reading a book or spending her free time at the swimming pool. They definitely didn't have very much in common—except a physical fitness demerit.

Even though she'd never visited her in

cabin seven before, Sarah decided to see if Liza was there. The cabin door was open a little and Sarah leaned close until she heard voices.

"Don't worry, Liza," Samantha said. "One demerit isn't going to get you in trouble."

"But it was embarrassing," Liza complained. "I don't see why she had to make such a big deal about it in front of everyone."

"I know," Samantha agreed. "I think it's embarrassing when she tells us to try harder, too. I *am* trying hard."

Sarah couldn't believe her perfect timing. She tapped lightly on the wooden door, and Liza looked up. She and Samantha were playing Yahtzee on the floor.

"Come on in, Sarah," Liza said, sounding a little surprised. "Why aren't you with your cabin mates?"

"Or alone reading?" Samantha added.

"I didn't really want to be cooped up in a cabin listening to Alison's pets talk about how great she is." Sarah decided not to mention the incident in the woods with Alison.

"Don't you and your sister get along?" Liza asked.

Sarah shrugged. "We're usually not around

each other much. And it's probably not a good idea to hang around Sunnyside together." She looked directly at the two girls. "I don't want people to think she's showing any favoritism toward me—like with the other cabin six girls," she said pointedly.

Sarah felt a little guilty since she *had* wanted Alison to let her off easier at first. But not anymore. That was too much to hope for. Now she just wanted her to stop picking on her.

Liza and Samantha stopped playing their game. "You think she's purposely favoring the cabin six girls?" Liza asked.

"She's been kind of strict with everyone else—with demerits and everything," Sarah replied.

Liza looked at Samantha and then at Sarah. "Yeah, we were just talking about how tough she was on you and me today, but I wasn't going to say anything since she's your sister," Liza said.

"She just gave me that demerit because I wasn't going along with her—like the others do. They worship her like she's some kind of a Greek goddess," Sarah said, trying to look especially disgusted. "But I think she's just abusing her power. I don't want to be part of it."

"She does sort of ignore us. Who knows, I might be the next one in line for a demerit," Samantha said. Liza nodded.

Talking about Alison with people who actually agreed with her was making her feel better. Suddenly a thought struck her. "I have an idea." Sarah's eyes gleamed. "If we're just going to get demerits anyway, let's make it really worthwhile."

"What do you mean?" Liza asked.

"Alison's having her fun at our expense. Why don't we have a little fun with her?"

Liza and Samantha looked at her with interest. Sarah continued. "During breaks, we could talk about how much we hate the class—so that *everyone* can hear."

"Yeah, and we can let the air out of all the balls one night," Samantha suggested.

"How about if we accidentally trip and fall a lot during the exercises?" Liza giggled.

"And when we play games, we can be really bad and purposely make mistakes. Alison can't say anything as long as we're playing," Samantha added.

Sarah hesitated. Was this going too far? She

had never purposely acted up in a class before—not even a class she didn't like. "But if
we do that, our team will lose," she reminded
Samantha.

"No it won't. This is the team I'm playing
for!" Liza and Samantha slapped each other
a high five.

Sarah was a little frightened at how quickly
the ideas had come. Even though she sometimes played pranks on Alison at home, she'd
never actually *plotted* against her before. She
wondered if Alison had ever been angry
enough at her to gang up with other people
against her. Luckily, the only other person
around was their father, so Sarah had never
had to find out. Sarah wasn't sure how she
felt about conspiring against her own sister.

But it was too late to think about all that
now. The thrill of finally having people on her
side outweighed her doubts. She had thought
of the plan and gotten other people excited
about it. She couldn't back out now.

After free time, Sarah walked back to her
cabin. Megan met her at the door. "I've been
looking all over for you. I was imagining all
sorts of horrible things had happened to you,"
she scolded.

Sarah shrugged. "Why were you so worried? I go off by myself all the time," she reminded her.

"Not into the woods. Alison told me she found you there," Megan said.

"And she gave me a demerit for it. Can you believe it? Carolyn never would have."

"Probably not if she knew you were really upset," Megan agreed.

"Plus, if I get one more demerit, I can't go to Pine Ridge."

"I'm sure you don't have anything to worry about. You've never gotten three demerits in one week before," Megan reminded her.

But then, Alison had never been around before, Sarah thought. She wondered what Megan would think of her plan. "Well, maybe I can make Alison regret giving me two," she said.

Megan looked at Sarah suspiciously. "What do you mean?"

"I was just in cabin seven with Liza and Samantha. They don't like the way they're being treated either, so we came up with a plan," Sarah explained. "We'll do everything that Alison wants us to do. We'll just do a few things she doesn't want us to do." Sarah took a deep breath and looked Megan in the eye. "Do you want to go along with us? It'd be great."

Sarah wasn't actually sure it would be so great, but she knew that if Megan decided to join in the plan, at least she wouldn't feel so alone. She liked having Liza and Samantha on her side, but adding another cabin six girl would make the gang complete. It would also help her feel that what she was doing was okay.

"I don't know, Sarah." Megan hesitated. "It's not really fair to Alison to act up like that since she hasn't really done anything wrong. You know the counselors are *supposed* to give you a demerit for going into the woods alone. Alison was just following the rules."

"It doesn't bother me that much that the others are siding against me, but you're my best friend!" Sarah complained.

"Sarah . . . but . . ." Megan tried to apologize, but Sarah wouldn't let her.

"I've heard enough excuses from Alison, Megan. I don't need to hear them from you, too," Sarah snapped and pushed her way past Megan into the cabin.

The rest of the day, Sarah tried to keep a

distance from her cabin mates. She had had her fill of confrontations for one afternoon. As lonely as she was, not spending time with her friends had one obvious advantage. For the first time since Alison showed up at Sunnyside, Sarah had a chance to finish her book.

Avoiding her cabin mates was a little more difficult the following day. Sarah had to eat breakfast, clean up the cabin for inspection, and go to swimming class with them, but she spoke to them only if they said something to her first—and even then she tried not to say too much. She didn't like being cold, but Alison had definitely caused a rift between her and the other girls, and Sarah knew that any conversation was a potential argument. And nothing made Sarah feel worse than arguing with her friends.

At lunch, Trina started talking about her parents again. "I just don't understand why I haven't heard from them!"

"Why don't you ask Ms. Winkle if you can use her phone?" Katie suggested to Trina. "I bet she'll make an exception this time."

Trina picked at her lunch. "What excuse will I use?"

"Tell her you're homesick," Megan said.

"She'd never believe that after three years I suddenly became homesick," Trina reminded her.

"Why don't you just tell her that you think something horrible has happened to your mother?" Erin asked.

Trina's face became as white as a sheet. "Erin!" Katie shouted. "That was a stupid thing to say!"

"I'm sorry. I didn't mean that I really thought it was true. I just thought it would be a good excuse," Erin said quickly.

"I'm sure nothing's happened to your mother," Megan said reassuringly. "Someone would have gotten in touch with you by now." Trina nodded slightly.

Sarah wished she could forget her pride and help her friends comfort Trina. Then she remembered that no one had rushed to her aid the day before when she stormed out of the cabin into the pouring rain. If they want me as a friend, they'll have to come get me!

Sarah had worn her physical fitness clothes to lunch so she didn't have to go back to the cabin to change. But she lingered outside with Samantha and Liza, so they were still the last ones to arrive in class—just as they'd planned it. They weren't late, though, so Alison couldn't give them demerits.

Sarah did all the exercises, but she didn't work as hard as she could have. Whenever Alison wasn't watching her, Sarah stopped doing the exercises. But just before she thought Alison would look in her direction, she tried to look especially intense and started to do the exercise.

"Nice job, Sarah!" Alison said. Liza giggled and gave Sarah a thumbs-up.

When everyone was supposed to count out loud, the girls took turns saying the wrong numbers. They managed to confuse the rest of the class.

"Why are you doing this?" Megan whispered to Sarah.

Sarah put her finger to her lips. "Shhh! No talking." She looked at Liza and Samantha and snickered.

"Oww!" Liza screamed and fell to the ground during the high knee kicks. She grabbed her ankle and rolled on the ground, distorting her face. All the girls rushed to her side.

Alison pushed through the circle of onlook-

80

ers. Her eyes were the size of saucers. "Are you okay?" she asked. Alison was genuinely concerned—and frightened. Sarah began to think that maybe they'd gone a little too far.

"Oh, sure," Liza said as she stood up without any problem. "I guess I just landed on it wrong."

Alison looked puzzled. "Okay, get back in your spots everyone." She stared directly at Liza. "False alarm."

As Sarah moved back into her spot, she whispered to Liza and Samantha, "That's enough for today."

But after that, no one could concentrate. The class was so distracted that the girls frequently forgot Alison's instructions or got confused about which direction they were supposed to be stepping. Some of them were even doing the wrong exercises.

"Okay, I guess everybody's pretty tired today," Alison said. "We'll stop a little early."

As soon as class was over, the cabin six girls gathered around Sarah.

"What was going on in there?" Megan asked.

"I *told* you," Sarah said. "Samantha and

Liza and I are going to give Alison a little trouble. Like she's giving us."

"She's not giving *me* any trouble," Erin remarked.

"Well, lucky you," Sarah snapped.

"I don't get it," Trina said. "You've never been friends with Samantha and Liza before."

Sarah sniffed. "Yeah, well, I had a pretty good feeling you guys wouldn't go along with me on this."

"Of course we wouldn't," Erin replied. "We *like* Alison."

"That's your problem," Sarah muttered.

Katie put her hands on her hips. "Sarah, this is stupid! I think you're being very childish. And you're ruining the class for the rest of us!"

Sarah faced her with cold eyes. "That's tough!" And she turned away. "Hey, Liza, where are you going?"

"Arts and crafts."

"Wait up, I'll go with you." And without another word to her cabin mates, she ran off with Liza.

"We were great today!" Liza said with enthusiasm. "And I don't think Alison had a clue!"

Sarah smiled grimly. They went into the arts and crafts cabin, where Liza headed for a particular table with pottery lying on it. "Keep me company while I paint this."

As Sarah sat in the chair next to Liza, her mind wandered. It was pretty boring to sit and watch someone else work on painting a pot.

As Sarah looked to the door of the cabin, Katie came in. And Alison was right behind her.

Darn, Sarah thought, I'd forgotten Alison was going to help Katie with her rug. She tried to look engrossed in what Liza was doing and hoped they hadn't seen her, too. After class, Sarah wasn't quite ready to face either one of them.

No such luck! Sarah felt her sister walking toward her. "Hi, Liza. Hi, Sarah." She smiled.

"Oh, hi," Sarah said looking at the pot again.

"Katie and I are going to work on her rug."

"Okay," Sarah said, hoping Alison would get the hint. She hovered for what seemed like at least a minute longer.

"That's going to be a beautiful bowl, Liza," Alison commented.

"Thanks," Liza mumbled without looking up.

"You know, Sarah, maybe you should take up a craft like pottery or weaving." Alison smiled at her sister.

Sarah was tired of being compared to the other girls. Alison and Katie might think those were interesting activities, but Sarah definitely was *not* interested. Alison was always trying to persuade her to do something other than reading or writing—just because Alison didn't like to do those things. "I'm not interested in pottery or weaving," Sarah snapped.

"Come on, Alison. My rug's over here," Katie said coldly. Alison said, " 'Bye, Sarah and Liza," and walked away.

Sarah couldn't stand the tension with her cabin mates, but what could she do? Every time she tried to get back at Alison for picking on her, she upset her friends. Sarah knew that after the way Alison had treated her, she had a right to get revenge, but no one except Liza and Samantha understood that.

She was even more determined to see her plan through. It wasn't her fault Alison had caused so much trouble. But for the sake of peace in cabin six, it was up to her to see that Alison didn't stay around to cause any more problems. She would have her friends all to herself once her sister was gone. Until then, life at Sunnyside couldn't get back to normal.

Chapter 7

Sarah ate dinner with Liza and Samantha that evening. "I've come up with another idea for Operation Torture Alison," she said, swallowing a meatball.

Liza rubbed her hands together demonically. "Ooo! I can't wait to hear it. I had so much fun in class today."

"Tonight we'll all go to the camp fire with our cabins. At 7:30 meet me by the camp fire. Once it's safe to sneak away, we'll go to the counselors' cabin. Everyone will be so busy talking to Eagle boys and listening to the music that no one will notice we're gone."

"What do we do when we get there?" Samantha asked.

Sarah reached into her shorts pocket and pulled out a handful of small silver packets.

"I took a bunch of syrup packets at breakfast this morning. There are about twenty more of these under my pillow in the cabin."

Liza and Samantha scrunched their noses and looked confused. Did she have to explain everything? "We'll sneak into the counselors' cabin and empty these into the foot of Alison's bed," Sarah whispered. "She'll slide into bed and get a gooey surprise!"

"Gross!" The two girls squealed.

"Exactly." Sarah smiled. "She won't know what hit her."

"But didn't Carolyn see you bring the syrup back to your cabin?" Liza asked. "She'll know you did it when Alison reports it at the next counselors' meeting."

"Don't worry. I went back through the breakfast line a few times this morning," Sarah began. "Everyone in cabin six thought I was doing it to get away from them, so no one followed me. Plus, I wore my baggy sweatshirt with the big pocket in front. No one could tell I had anything in it."

"We could get in big trouble for ruining camp property," Samantha reminded her.

"The syrup'll wash right out. Haven't you ever spilled some on yourself?"

Liza raised her eyebrows in approval. "It sounds foolproof to me," she said. Samantha agreed.

Sarah met the cabin seven girls by the camp fire as planned. Even though it was pretty dark in the rest of the camp, the glow from the flames lit up the activity around the camp fire. Music poured out from the stereo as campers from Sunnyside and Eagle mingled and laughed.

Erin and Bobby danced in an open area near the fire. Megan, Trina, and Katie roasted marshmallows on long sticks over the fire as Carolyn and Alison each dropped burnt blobs into their mouths.

No one noticed when Sarah, Samantha, and Liza slipped away to the counselors' cabin.

"This must be Alison's," Sarah said pointing to a neatly made bed. "I recognize her trunk."

Liza nervously tugged her brown bangs. "We better do this fast," she said. "Someone might come back early."

"Okay, okay," Sarah said, emptying the contents of her huge pocket onto the floor. "Everybody start pouring."

Sarah pulled back the sheets. The three girls furiously opened the packages and dumped them into the bed.

"Yuck! I'm getting syrup all over me," Samantha complained.

"Keep going," Sarah encouraged her. "It's for a worthy cause." But as she continued, Sarah wasn't sure how worthy a cause it really was. Her fingers were sore from all the ripping, and syrup was all over her hands, face, arms, and hair. She couldn't wait to get back to the cabin to take a shower.

"Listen!" Liza whispered. "Someone's coming."

"I didn't hear anything," Sarah said.

"I heard it too!" Samantha hissed. "We'd better hide!"

Sarah's heart raced as she grabbed the empty packets and slid under one of the counselors' beds. She held her breath and waited.

After what seemed like ages, Samantha said, "Nobody's coming."

Liza giggled. "I guess it was a squirrel or something."

Sarah looked at her in annoyance. "Come on. Let's make the bed and get out of here." But she couldn't help smiling as she pulled the quilt over the slimy mess. What a great revenge!

"You want to come back to cabin seven with us?" Liza asked Sarah. "Maybe we could come up with something good to do to Alison's precious pets."

"Huh?"

"Your cabin mates!"

Sarah hesitated. She really wasn't in the mood to hang out with Samantha and Liza. Except when they were plotting against Alison, they were really kind of boring.

Besides, that last comment of Liza's bothered her. It was one thing to play pranks on Alison. But even though she wasn't at all happy with her cabin mates, the thought of playing pranks on *them* made her uneasy. Alison probably wouldn't retaliate, but she wasn't so certain about cabin six. Besides, in spite of everything, the cabin six girls were her friends. Once Alison left camp, Sarah would be doing pranks *with* cabin six, not *to* them.

Sarah didn't want to hurt Liza's and Samantha's feelings by admitting she'd rather write her father a long overdue letter.

"I'm pretty tired," she lied, licking syrup

off her finger. "I'm just going to clean up and go to sleep."

Just as Sarah was signing her letter to her father, she heard Carolyn's voice at the cabin door. "Don't forget the counselors' meeting tomorrow," she said. Sarah figured Carolyn must be talking to Alison. The two counselors spent all their spare time together—whenever Alison wasn't with Trina, Erin, Katie, or Megan, that is. She thought about what she and the cabin seven girls had done to Alison's bed and shivered.

"I'll be at the meeting. See you tomorrow, girls," Alison said cheerfully.

"Night, Alison," Sarah's cabin mates chorused.

Sarah stuck the letter into an envelope and shoved it under her pillow and then pretended to be asleep. Her cabin mates filed in the door, laughing.

Carolyn said, "I'll see you guys in the morning," and shut her door.

"That was definitely the best camp fire yet," Erin said dreamily.

"You and Bobby looked like you were having a great time," Megan said.

"Yeah, you were the only ones slow dancing," Katie pointed out. "Weren't you afraid he'd catch your rash? Or that you'd catch whatever disease makes him so goofy?"

Erin huffed. "Very funny. You don't *catch* a rash," she said. "Besides, my rash is gone. The stuff Alison gave me worked."

"Shh! Sarah's asleep," Trina whispered to the other girls.

"Let's go brush our teeth and talk about tonight," Megan suggested as they tiptoed into the bathroom.

A sickening feeling sat in the pit of Sarah's stomach. Maybe I'm not being fair to them. After all, they're not holding a grudge against me.

But it was easy for them to be nice to Sarah when she was asleep. The problem was being nice to her when she was awake—and Alison was around. Sarah wasn't ready to forget the way they'd been treating her. And they'd continue treating her that way until they didn't have Alison brainwashing them.

The next day, swimming class was a free swim. Erin floated leisurely on a raft while Trina, Katie, and Megan practiced lifesaving techniques. The best way for Sarah to avoid them was to practice diving off the diving board. She preferred swimming, but she didn't want to risk having to talk to them.

Sarah stood at the end of the line for the diving board behind two girls from another cabin.

"Did you see what Alison Fine was wearing this morning at breakfast?" Sarah overheard one of them say.

"Yeah, she looked great. Let's face it. Alison is perfect. I bet she's never done anything wrong in her life. I hope I'm that cool when I'm in college."

Unfortunately, Sarah hadn't seen her sister at breakfast even though she'd kept her eye out for the sticky victim. Alison had probably arrived after Sarah left the dining hall because she'd spent the morning showering gooey globs of syrup out of her toes. But from the sound of things, she'd managed to clean it all up.

Sarah put her hand up to her mouth and snickered as she thought about all the stories she could tell that would destroy Alison's perfect image. Hey! Why not?

Sarah leaned forward and poked her head

between the two girls. "She wasn't too cool the night my dad caught her making out in our driveway!" Sarah said loud enough for everyone to hear—including Darrell and the cabin six girls.

"Really? That's funny." Three more girls joined the group and no one was worried about losing her place in line for the diving board.

"Hey, Sally," a girl called to her friend in the pool. "You've got to come hear this."

"Of course, private humiliation is nothing compared to public embarrassment," Sarah continued. "Her face was bright red the night she tripped and fell during her dance routine for community talent night." She threw back her head and laughed with the others. Sarah had felt horrible the night it happened, but the excitement she was feeling at that moment made her forget. Finally, people were listening to her.

Sarah went on and on with the stories, sometimes stretching the truth just enough to make them really funny—and to bring Alison down another notch in the audience's opinion.

Sarah looked smugly at her cabin six friends, who had stopped what they had been doing to listen with shocked expressions.

Megan shot Sarah a disgusted look before turning away. "Come on, you guys," she said to the others. "Let's work on our back stroke."

Sarah missed her best friend and couldn't stand the fact that Megan was obviously so disappointed in her. But it felt great that people were finally listening to the truth about the real, imperfect Alison. Besides, once Alison was gone and the old gang was together again, Sarah was certain Megan and the others would forget all about the conniving she'd had to do.

By afternoon, the sun was out, the ground had almost completely dried up, and the water on the lake had settled. Although she hadn't spoken with them at all that day, Sarah knew that during free time her cabin mates would be horseback riding or canoeing, so it would be safe for her to sneak into the cabin to see if she could find a book.

She'd already read everything in her library at least once, but maybe Carolyn would have something new that she could borrow. Even if her counselor didn't have anything, it had been so long since she'd opened a book, rereading a novel was better than trying to come up with something else to do.

As she headed to the cabin, Sarah kept an eye out for her cabin mates and Alison. I'm sure they're off somewhere listening to Alison go on and on about what a wonderful human being she is, Sarah thought.

She was still so angry at the thought of Alison's spending free time with *her* friends that she almost didn't notice the voices coming out of cabin six. Sarah stood frozen.

"I told my mom I wouldn't come to Sunnyside this summer if she needed me at home," Trina said. "I guess she really doesn't need me at all."

"There could be a lot of good reasons you haven't heard from your parents," Alison assured her.

"I've gone over it a million times in my head, Alison. My dad said he might not have time to send me a note from Japan. And even if he mailed a postcard the day he got there, I wouldn't have received it by now," Trina explained.

"Well?" Alison encouraged her.

"But my mom hasn't gone out of town and even when she's really busy, she sends me a piece of paper with a smiling face or something," Trina told the counselor. "Maybe I shouldn't have deserted her and come here. Maybe she's angry at me for not staying home."

"Do you honestly believe that's what your mother wants?"

"I don't know," Trina said sadly. Sarah didn't move a muscle during the long pause that followed. "I thought it was pretty lonely being an only child, but that's nothing compared to having only one parent all the time."

"I'm sure your parents' divorce has been a big adjustment for you," Alison said quietly. "But just because your parents don't live together doesn't mean they're each not there for you."

"I guess I'm being pretty selfish. My mom's the one who should be complaining," Trina sighed. Sarah couldn't believe her ears. Trina was the last person on earth she'd call selfish. "My dad has a new girlfriend. He brought her here for Parents' Day. But my mom doesn't have anybody."

"Sure she does, Trina. She's got you. You'd be surprised how far a daughter's love can travel. You don't have to be standing next to her for her to know you love her."

There was a moment of silence before Trina spoke again. "Thanks, Alison. I guess I was so busy feeling sorry for my mom, I started feeling sorrier for myself."

"See ya later."

Sarah heard Erin's bed creak; then, footsteps approached the door and paused. She raced as lightly as she could to the back of the cabin and crouched down. She stretched her neck to peek around the corner and saw Alison walking away from cabin six toward the counselors' cabin. The girls at swimming class had been right. Alison looked perfect. No signs of maple syrup anywhere.

While she squatted against the wall outside the cabin, Sarah grew more jealous thinking about what she'd overheard. She remembered all the great heart-to-heart talks she and Alison had at home and on the phone. But now that she needed Alison's advice more than ever, she couldn't get it. *Alison* was the problem!

But Sarah couldn't blame Trina for looking up to Alison. Alison did do a great job helping people work out their feelings.

She heard Katie, Megan, and Erin coming toward the cabin from the opposite direction. As they got closer, Sarah could see them, but a bush concealed her.

They were laughing. She couldn't hear what they were laughing about, but it didn't matter. Waves of misery passed over her.

Already, she missed her cabin mates. She didn't like being mad at them, and she hated having them mad at her. Liza and Samantha were no substitute for cabin six girls.

It was all Alison's fault. *She* had come between Sarah and her cabin mates. It wasn't right. Sarah might have to suffer through physical fitness class, but she shouldn't have to suffer all the time.

Maybe it was time to make up with her cabin mates. She'd call off the class pranks. She was still upset with Alison, but she just wouldn't discuss it in front of her friends.

She marched into the cabin. "Hi guys," she said. "What's up?"

They all stopped talking and looked at her uneasily. Sarah ambled over to Erin's bed and flopped down as if nothing had happened.

But they were all still staring at her. Sarah

was going to have to offer some sort of excuse for her behavior.

"Listen, you guys, I know I've been acting goofy. I guess it's just my mood."

"Have you made up with your sister?" Megan asked.

"Oh, don't worry about that. It's no big deal," Sarah lied. "Hey, does anyone know what we're having for dinner?"

"I think it's spaghetti and meatballs," Trina said.

"All-right!" Sarah yelled, with a lot more enthusiasm than she felt.

"It's fattening," Erin complained. "I'm not eating the meatballs."

"Good," Sarah said. "I'll eat yours."

Erin looked pointedly at Sarah's stomach. "I said, they're fattening."

Sarah grinned. "Then we'll split them between us. Okay, guys?"

They were still eyeing her oddly, but at least Megan was smiling and nodding. Sarah smiled back.

She knew her problems weren't over. But at least, here in the cabin, things were almost back to normal.

Chapter 8

Sarah was careful not to say anything negative about physical fitness class the next morning. She felt a little silly suddenly pretending everything was fine, but she didn't want to say anything that might start an argument. Most of her comments were limited to vague observations like "I guess we'll be outside today" or "I wonder if we'll be doing stretching exercises."

"It'll be great having the whole field to use, won't it, Sarah?" Trina asked.

"Oh, yes. Physical fitness will probably be twice as much fun"—which wasn't saying much since nothing times two is still nothing!

"We better get going. Are you coming with us or waiting for Liza and Samantha?" Megan asked as Sarah unrolled a brand-new pair of socks.

"Oh, I don't think I'll be going to class with them anymore." Sarah smiled. "Just let me put my tennis shoes on and I'll be ready." Sarah pulled the shoes on her feet and stood up. The girls walked together to the field for physical fitness.

"Oh, neat, Erin. Who taught you to braid a ribbon into your hair like that?" Megan asked.

"Alison, of course. No one else at this camp knows the first thing about hair fashion," Erin responded.

"That's because most of us don't dress like we're going to a dress-up party for physical fitness," Katie quipped.

It was great to be back with the cabin six gang again. Sarah almost forgot how much she dreaded facing her tyrant sister. Unfortunately, that wasn't the only thing she forgot. As she looked at Erin's braid with the pink ribbon running through it, she stopped dead in her tracks and grabbed a chunk of the loose hair falling over her shoulders and down her back.

"Oh my gosh," she gasped.

"What's wrong?" Megan asked.

"I forgot to pull my hair back," Sarah exclaimed as she ran back toward the cabin. One of Alison's rules was that any hair below the shoulders had to be pulled back.

"Don't worry!" Megan shouted behind her. "You've got plenty of time."

Sarah tore her part of the cabin apart looking for something to tie her ponytail with. "What could I have done with *all* those elastics?" she asked herself, tossing dirty laundry from one side of the room to the other.

Finally, she remembered Erin's neat box of hair accessories and hoped she wouldn't mind if Sarah borrowed a barrette. Sarah opened the box and grabbed the French one Alison had complimented the day she arrived at Sunnyside. Maybe Alison would like it just as much in her hair. She ran out the door and tried to make up for lost time.

By the time Sarah made it to the grassy section where everyone else was lined up, she was out of breath and tired. She slid into her spot.

"I'm sorry, Samantha, but you know you're not supposed to wear cleats to this class," Alison apologized gently. "That's a demerit, but

since it's your first, you don't have anything
to worry about."

Sarah saw Liza grin at her. Oh, no! Samantha had worn the cleats as part of the plan to
annoy Alison. Sarah had forgotten to tell
them she'd decided to call it off. They probably thought I was late on purpose too.

"You're late today, Sarah," Alison went on.
"That means another demerit.

Sarah stared at her, totally aghast. "But
that's three demerits I'll have this week! That
means I won't be able to go to Pine Ridge!"

She could have sworn she saw a glimpse of
sympathy in Alison's eyes. But it was gone
before she could be sure.

"I'm sorry, Sarah. But I can't bend the rules
for you."

Sarah was speechless. She'd been so looking forward to going to Pine Ridge and hitting
the bookstore. How could Alison do this to
her?

This was the limit. The absolute limit. She
turned her back on Alison and began walking
away.

Alison probably knew all along how much
I wanted to go to Pine Ridge to get those
books, she thought furiously. She gave me all

those demerits to keep me from reading. Well, I'll show her.

She could hear Alison's voice. "Trina, lead the warm-up stretches, please. I'll be right back."

It didn't take long for Alison to catch up to Sarah, but Sarah looked straight ahead and continued walking.

"You're not supposed to leave class without my permission," Alison reprimanded Sarah.

Sarah stopped and threw her arms in the air. "Why don't you just take your act somewhere else—far away?" Sarah asked.

"Sarah, I don't think I have to tell you the penalty for talking back to a counselor—not to mention completely ignoring her instructions," Alison said sternly.

"I wish you'd make up your mind. Either be the great camp counselor or everybody's friend."

"Can't I be both?" Alison asked.

"Not to me!" Sarah shouted. "I don't need friends like you." Her voice began to shake. Had she really just said that to Alison?

Alison looked shocked. "What are you talking about?" she asked, grabbing Sarah's arm.

"You're always so happy to see me when I come home at breaks."

"Well, I'm not happy to see you this time. In fact, I'll be happy when you're gone and I'll never have to see you again!"

The tears poured out of Sarah's eyes as she pulled her arm out of her sister's grasp and ran off.

Alone in her cabin, Sarah became more and more angry as she thought about how cruel Alison had been. But what could she do? Alison was determined to make Sarah miserable. And there was no doubt about it—in the battle of wills, Alison was winning. And she'd keep on winning, all summer long.

Suddenly the solution to the problem hit Sarah like a bolt of lightning. She'd always been great at problem solving but this seemed way too easy—and incredibly brilliant.

What if Ms. Winkle thought Alison was a terrible counselor? Sarah thought. Bye-bye, Alison—and physical fitness! She searched around the cabin for pieces of paper, pens, pencils, and Magic Markers.

Sarah tore the scrap paper into smaller pieces. On one slip, she wrote, "I think Alison plays favorites." On another she printed, "Alison is ruining Camp Sunnyside morale. She should leave."

Sarah continued scribbling on scraps of paper, varying the handwriting and message on each. She even used bad grammar and misspelled words on a few so it would look like the younger kids had contributed. She folded the notes and counted them: seventeen.

That should be enough to send Miss Perfect home!

Sarah was so pleased with her plan, she practically skipped to the suggestion box next to the dining hall. She shoved each note into the slit in the top.

When she had finished, Sarah turned to go back to the cabin. She saw Trina and Megan coming toward her.

Even though she felt a little awkward about the scene she'd created in class, Sarah decided to pretend nothing had happened. "What's up?" she asked.

"Alison let everyone out a little early," Megan explained. "She looked pretty upset about what happened, so we stayed after to talk to her."

The news that Alison was upset was music to Sarah's ears. "Did she brag about how much she liked giving me demerits? Or did she just tell you how surprised she was that I didn't believe her silly threats?" Sarah asked sarcastically.

Trina hung her head. "Actually, she told us she's going to leave Camp Sunnyside," she said. "She thinks she's ruining your summer, and that's the last thing she wanted."

"She's on her way to Ms. Winkle's office to resign," Megan added.

Sarah was stunned. Here was the news she'd been waiting for. It was too good to be true. Too bad she'd wasted time writing those notes.

Then her eyes narrowed. Maybe it really *was* too good to be true. Maybe Alison was just trying to make her feel guilty. Maybe her own cabin mates were lying, to make her feel kind toward Alison.

"I don't believe you," she said flatly.

Katie shrugged. "Go over to Ms Winkle's office and see for yourself."

"I just might do that." She ambled away, until she knew the others couldn't see her. Then she ran.

Sure enough, Alison was in the reception

room just outside Ms. Winkle's office. "What are you doing here?" Sarah asked.

"I'm going to give Ms. Winkle my resignation," Alison replied quietly.

"Oh." That was all Sarah needed to hear. Now she could leave. But something in Alison's face held her back. She couldn't remember ever seeing her sister look so sad. Drawing herself up stiffly, she asked, "Why did you suddenly decide to leave?"

"Because I didn't come here to make your life miserable. And I can see that's what I'm doing."

"I thought you were enjoying every minute of making my life miserable."

"Oh, Sarah, no!" Alison rose. "I see now that I came down too hard on you. I guess I was trying not to show favoritism, and I went overboard."

"You certainly did," Sarah said.

"Well, I'm sorry," Alison said. "That's all I can say. And now I'm leaving."

Sarah swallowed hard. "But . . . you won't have a summer job. What about the computer you were saving up for?"

Alison shrugged. "No computer is worth losing the love of a sister."

Sarah could feel the tears welling up in her own eyes. Looking into Alison's eyes, she wasn't sure if it was her own tears that were making Alison's eyes look blurry or if those were Alison's tears.

"It's my fault too," Sarah blurted out. "I wouldn't have behaved so badly with any other counselor."

"I guess we've both been silly," Alison said.

Sarah nodded. "I—I wish we could start all over."

"Me too."

They were both silent for a minute.

"I'm really sorry, Sarah," Alison whispered.

"Yeah. I'm sorry too," Sarah replied.

Alison smiled slightly. "That's okay. But you're lucky I didn't make you do my laundry."

"What do you mean?" Sarah asked.

"Do you have any idea how many times I had to wash those sheets to get the syrup out?" The girls burst out laughing. Alison put her arms around Sarah, and Sarah hugged her back.

Ms. Winkle opened her door as the sisters let go of each other. "Who's next?" she asked.

"Alison or . . . uh . . . um . . ." Even after three years, Ms. Winkle couldn't remember Sarah's name.

Sarah looked at Alison and then at Ms. Winkle. "I don't think we need to see you anymore," Sarah said. Ms. Winkle looked puzzled when Alison agreed. She shook her head and went back into her office.

They stepped outside. "Today's a really nice day," Sarah observed. "Maybe we should go on a hike."

"Sarah, you don't want to go on a hike any more than I want to sit in a cabin reading a book all day."

"I guess you're right," Sarah agreed. Then she stopped dead in her tracks. "Oh my gosh!" she exclaimed.

"What is it?" Alison asked.

"Oh, it's just that I remembered it's supposed to be quiet time and I have to get back to the cabin. I'll see you later," she said.

Sarah did have to get back to the cabin quickly, but it wasn't quiet time she was worried about. She needed help getting the notes out of the suggestion box before Ms. Winkle found them.

Carolyn would be in her room during quiet

time. All campers had to stay in their cabins, and there was supposed to be absolutely no talking. Breaking the rules carried a heavy penalty. Sarah didn't want to have to miss *two* field trips, but she was desperate, and she really needed her friends' help.

Getting those notes out of the suggestion box was more important than anything else at that moment. After all she'd been through, she had to make sure *no one* saw those complaints.

"You guys, we've gotta talk," Sarah whispered as she ran into the cabin.

Katie put her finger to her mouth. "Shh!" she said, gesturing with her head toward Carolyn's room.

Sarah motioned for everyone to come closer. She sat on the edge of Erin's bed where Erin sat filing her nails. Katie, Trina, and Megan huddled on the floor in front of her.

"Don't worry about being gone during quiet time," Trina said. "I told Carolyn what happened in physical fitness class. I hope that was okay."

"Thanks, Trina." She looked at her cabin mates' curious faces. "Alison's going to stay," she told them.

"Yay!" Megan yelled and slapped her hand over her mouth.

"Is everything going to be okay between you two?" Trina asked.

"Yeah, I think we both just needed time to adjust to the idea of being together here." Sarah remembered the reason she needed to talk to her friends in the first place and panicked. "I really need your help, though, or things could blow up again." She explained how she'd written up all the notes and put them in the suggestion box.

Erin dropped her nail file onto the bed. "We've got to do something *right away!*" she said.

"Teddy left a screwdriver here the other day when he came to fix the shower," Katie reminded them. "Maybe you could use it to pry the latch off the box."

"It's worth a try," Megan whispered. "I'll go with you." They hurried out of the cabin.

Luckily, Sarah and Megan made it to the dining hall without anyone's seeing them. Megan placed the screwdriver under the latch and pulled the screws out. Sarah could hardly contain her excitement. All she needed to do was grab the notes, and they'd be home free.

As she reached inside the box to grab the stack of papers, Sarah felt a presence behind her. Megan was right next to her, which meant a third person had joined them. Slowly she and Megan turned around and saw Alison standing behind them.

How could Sarah have put Megan and Alison in this awkward position? What a mess! Sarah inhaled deeply and prepared to defend her best friend.

Just as she was about to tell Alison all about the notes she'd written, Alison smiled and said, "Teddy was wondering where he left that screwdriver. I'll take it to him. Thanks for returning it."

At first Sarah was too stunned to speak. Alison was actually trying to avoid giving them demerits. "Yeah, and you better tell him this box needs a little repair," Sarah suggested.

"Thanks for pointing that out," Alison said, sounding very serious.

"We better get back to the cabin," Megan suggested. "See you later, Alison."

Sarah and Megan started toward the cabin. "Wait! I almost forgot," Sarah said. She turned around and walked a few steps back to the suggestion box where Alison was still standing. "I almost forgot the papers I left here," she said, reaching into the box. She pulled the notes out and wadded them in her fist. Mission accomplished!

Megan and Sarah hurried back to the cabin. There were only ten minutes of quiet time left, and after it was over they all walked to the dining hall for dinner.

Once they were seated with their bowls of chili, Megan told Trina, Katie, and Erin all about the close call.

"Suddenly, a dark shadow hovered above us. The figure seemed to be covered in hair," Megan said, and Erin, Katie, and Trina leaned closer with their eyes wide open.

"Who was it?" Katie asked.

"What happened?" Erin said in an impatient voice.

"Alison." Megan shrugged and giggled.

"You dope," Trina teased. "You really had us going. She didn't . . . ?"

"Give us demerits?" Sarah asked. Trina nodded. "Nope. I really think she's starting to get the hang of being a counselor now."

Ms. Winkle stood up to make the dinner announcements and the tables of girls quieted down. "I'm afraid we have an embarrassing

117

situation on our hands," she began. "In all the confusion and excitement of the past couple weeks, I'm afraid one of the mail bags found its way into my closet."

Sarah wasn't the least bit surprised to hear that Ms. Winkle hadn't noticed a large bag of mail sitting in her closet for almost two weeks.

"Since I know you girls are eagerly awaiting these letters, you won't have to wait for the regular mail delivery," she continued. "I'll call out your cabin numbers, and one representative from each cabin should come and get the stack of mail."

The cabin six girls didn't need to discuss who would be collecting their mail. Trina looked like she would burst. But it was obvious to Sarah that she was trying not to look too excited—just in case.

When Ms. Winkle called cabin six, Trina shot up to the front of the dining hall like a light. She politely thanked Ms. Winkle and zipped back to her seat. Everyone got one piece of mail—except Trina. Her father missed her so much, he'd sent two postcards from Japan as soon as his plane landed. Plus, she pulled a five-page letter from her mother out of a pink envelope.

"You know, I think this is going to turn out to be the best Sunnyside summer yet," Sarah commented after Trina finished reading the letter out loud. "I'm glad Alison decided not to leave us."

"And we're glad you're acting like a cabin six girl again," Trina commented.

"Yeah, you had us pretty worried," Katie agreed.

"*I* had you worried? What about Trina. For the past two weeks, she's looked like one of those zombies Megan always thinks are hiding under her bed," Sarah said.

Megan's eyebrows narrowed. "I don't think zombies hide under my bed," she corrected Sarah.

Oh, no! Why couldn't Sarah keep her big mouth shut. Everyone was having such a good time and she'd found a way to ruin it by offending Megan.

Then Megan grinned. "They live behind the shower curtain."

The table erupted in laughter. Sarah leaned back in her chair and smiled happily. Everything was normal again. The fun times in cabin six had returned. And she made a promise to herself—never to do anything that might threaten their happiness again.

Even if that meant doing calisthenics.

MEET THE GIRLS FROM CABIN SIX IN

(#13) BIG SISTER BLUES   76551-9 ($2.95 US/$3.50 Can)

(#12) THE TENNIS TRAP   76184-X ($2.95 US/$3.50 Can)

(#11) THE PROBLEM WITH PARENTS
76183-1 ($2.95 US/$3.50 Can)

(#10) ERIN AND THE MOVIE STAR 76181-5 ($2.95 US/$3.50 Can)

(#9) THE NEW-AND-IMPROVED SARAH
76180-7 ($2.95 US/$3.50 Can)

(#8) TOO MANY COUNSELORS   75913-6 ($2.95 US/$3.50 Can)

(#7) A WITCH IN CABIN SIX   75912-8 ($2.95 US/$3.50 Can)

(#6) KATIE STEALS THE SHOW   75910-1 ($2.95 US/$3.50 Can)

(#5) LOOKING FOR TROUBLE   75909-8 ($2.95 US/$3.50 Can)

(#4) NEW GIRL IN CABIN SIX   75703-6 ($2.95 US/$3.50 Can)

(#3) COLOR WAR!   75702-8 ($2.50 US/$2.95 Can)

(#2) CABIN SIX PLAYS CUPID   75701-X ($2.50 US/$2.95 Can)

(#1) NO BOYS ALLOWED!   75700-1 ($2.50 US/$2.95 Can)

MY CAMP MEMORY BOOK   76081-9 ($5.95 US/$7.95 Can)

CAMP SUNNYSIDE FRIENDS SPECIAL:
CHRISTMAS REUNION   76270-6 ($2.95 US/$3.50 Can)